Jurassic Jam

WORDS BY MARIA WEST
PICTURES BY CHRIS LENSCH

First published by Experience Early Learning Company
7243 Scotchwood Lane, Grawn, Michigan 49637 USA

Text Copyright © 2015 by Experience Early Learning Co.
Manufactured in No.8, Yin Li Street, Tian He District, Guangzhou,
Guangdong, China by Sun Fly Printing Limited
4th Printing 01/2023

ISBN: 978-1-937954-18-5
Visit us at www.ExperienceEarlyLearning.com

It was a hot and hip Jurassic night.
The sky was clear; the stars were bright.

The dinosaurs were having a dance.

INVITATION

DINOSAUR DANCE

TONIGHT

It was time to put on their fancy pants!

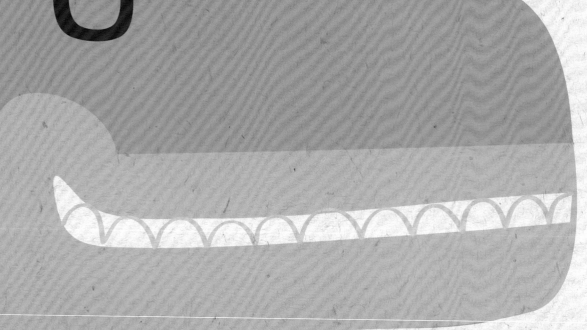
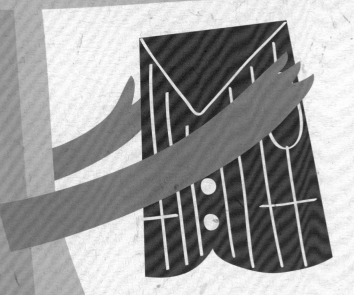

Allosaurus found his vest !

Brachiosaurus hemmed her dress.

They came from all across the land

to hear their favorite prehistoric band.

The crowd arrived.
The music was swinging.
It was time to start dancing,
laughing and singing.

Stegosaurus was plucking the bass:

Boom, Boom-ba,
Boom, Boom-ba.
Boom, Boom-ba,
Boom, Boom-ba.
Boom, Boom-ba,
Boom...

BOOM
BA

Pterodactyl was jamming on the drums:

Boom, bap,

boom boom bap.

Boom, bap,

boom boom bap.

Boom, bap,

boom boom...

**Tyrannosaurus rex
was strumming the guitar:**

Wikka, wikka, wak.
Wikka, wikka, wak.
Wikka, wikka...

Mussaurus was playing the organ:

Woo, woo, weeeeee.
Woo, woo, weeeeee.
Woo, woo...

Brontosaurus was blowing on the horn:

Bah bada, bow.
Bah bada, bow.
Bah bada...

**Triceratops was singing
sweet melodies:**

Doo, wop, dee, doo.
Doo, wop, dee, doo.
Doo, wop, dee...

Dinosaurs were gettin' down:

Twirl, shake, shake.
Twirl, shake, shake.
Twirl, shake...

They clapped their claws with a shimmy shake.

Their sweet moves made the dance floor quake.

As the Jurassic moon was
getting low,
the dancers swayed and the
beat was slow.

When the last note played,
the band waved goodbye.
And the dinosaurs stretched
and rubbed their eyes.

They tipped their hats
and smiled bright,
then headed off into
the night.

They would jam again very soon,
under a new Jurassic moon.

Brontosaurus

Mussaurus

Triceratops

Stegosaurus

experience
EARLY LEARNING

Pterodactyl

Experience Early Learning specializes in the development and publishing of research-based curriculum, books, music and authentic assessment tools for early childhood teachers and parents around the world. Our mission is to inspire children to experience learning through creative expression, play and open-ended discovery. We believe educational materials that invite children to participate with their whole self (mind, body and spirit) support on-going development and encourage children to become the authors of their own unique learning stories.

www.ExperienceEarlyLearning.com

Tyrannosaurus rex

Brachiosaurus

Allosaurus

Ankylosaurus